Kally H.

THE GREAT RABBIT RIP-OFF

The Great Rabbit Rip-Off

A McGURK MYSTERY
BY E. W. HILDICK
ILLUSTRATED BY LISL WEIL

MACMILLAN PUBLISHING CO., INC.
New York

CHERRYLAND MIDDLE SCHOOL LIBRARY

Copyright © 1976 E. W. Hildick
Illustrations copyright © 1977 Macmillan Publishing Co., Inc.

Macmillan Publishing Co., Inc.
866 Third Avenue, New York, N.Y. 10022
Collier Macmillan Canada, Ltd.
Originally published in England in 1976 under the title
The Great Rabbit Robbery
First American edition 1977
Printed in the United States of America
10 9 8 7 6 5 4 3 2 1

11-1-77

LIBRARY OF CONGRESS CATALOGING IN PUBLICATION DATA
Hildick, Edmund Wallace.   The great rabbit rip-off.
(A McGurk mystery)
    Edition of 1976 published under title: The great rabbit robbery. SUMMARY:
The McGurk Organization's four young detectives swing into action when
one of them is accused of defacing and then stealing all the ornamental clay
rabbits in the neighborhood. [1. Mystery and detective stories]   I. Weil, Lisl.
II. Title.   PZ7.H5463Gr3   [Fic]   76–46296
ISBN 0–02–743820–1

By the Same Author

Contents

THE GREAT RABBIT RIP-OFF

1 The Red-Nosed Rabbits

I spotted them as soon as I stepped out of the house that Friday morning.

At first I thought they were bright scraps of paper that had blown into the yard. Shiny orange-red. Candy wrappers, maybe.

Then I looked again and saw that they were the rabbits' noses.

"Well!" I thought. "I know about red-nosed reindeers at Christmas. But this is the first time I've heard about red-nosed rabbits at Easter."

So I went closer and bent over them, where Mom had placed them: one at either side of our nameplate stuck into the lawn. The nameplate read ROCK-

AWAY, and the rabbits were looking across it at each other.

Yes. Someone had painted their noses red all right. In fact one had been given such a thick coat of the paint that it still felt slightly sticky when I touched it.

The rabbits weren't real, of course. They were made out of a light-gray clay that had set hard. In fact they weren't very special even as ornaments. They were just a charity idea that Donny Towers had dreamed up for Easter. Donny is a social worker. He helps teenagers who have been in trouble with the law. Someone had given him a load of clay and he decided to make it into Easter bunnies. Then he sold them at a dollar each. Since the money was all going to a good cause—to help set up a summer camp for city kids—lots of people bought them. They put them out in their front yards to show they had contributed. In a way, the rabbits were nothing more special than charity stickers or buttons.

Even so, I wasn't sure I liked the idea of someone coming around painting their noses this way, without asking. I mean what if my parents thought I'd done it?

I was just going to turn back and let Mom know

right away, so she wouldn't get any wrong ideas, when a voice called out from the next yard:

"Hey! Joey! You seen *this?*"

It was Willie Sandowsky. He was bending over *his* rabbit. His own nose was nearly touching the rabbit's, which doesn't mean he was bending all that low. Willie has such a long nose that just a slight stoop is enough to have it nearly hitting the target. In fact if anyone ever decided to paint *Willie's* nose, they'd have to figure on using half a can.

But it was the rabbit's nose that had been painted, just like my pair.

"Did *you* do this?" Willie asked, looking up with a grin.

"I did *not!*" I said, very firmly.

"No? Well. It looks kinda funny," he said. "I like it better this way. And you do have a great sense of humor, Joey."

"If you think it's so funny," I said, "maybe you did it. And ours too. Huh?"

He blinked across at the rabbits in our yard. Then I could tell by the way his eyes went wide that it was as big a surprise to him as it had been to me.

"Gee!" he cried. "Hey! Wow!"

Then he broke up laughing.

"So all right," I said. "*You* didn't do it. *I* didn't do it. So it's a mystery."

That stopped him laughing.

"Hey, yeah!" he said. "Maybe we can make that the Organization's next case. You know how McGurk's been itching for a mystery to solve."

That reminded me. We were supposed to be on our way to a meeting of the McGurk Organization that very morning. "An extra-special meeting," McGurk had called it. I looked at my watch.

"Come on," I said. "We're late already."

Well, late or not, extra-special meeting or not, it took us about twice the normal time to get to McGurk's house that morning. The reason? The rabbits again.

Everywhere, in almost every front yard on the way, the Mystery Painter had been at work. Some of these rabbits had been given red noses, too. But there were also some that had had the tips of their ears painted instead, and some with just their tails reddened, or their front paws.

Willie thought it was the funniest thing since Bugs Bunny. I had to *drag* him along after a bit. And when we finally made it to McGurk's, he just collapsed. He did. He just flopped down on the grass and rolled over on his back, howling.

McGurk's rabbit had not been touched in any of the usual places. Its ears and nose and feet and tail were still the basic light-gray. But this time it was the eyes. Two bright red shiny beady eyes.

Even I had to laugh.

Then I pulled Willie to his feet and we went to the basement door, down the steps at the side of the house, where it said:

```
HEADQUARTERS
KEEP OUT

THE McGURK
ORGANIZATION
# * # *
PRIVATE INVESTIGATIONS
MYSTERIES SOLVED
PERSONS PROTECTED
MISSING PERSONS FOUND
```

Being officers of the Organization, we took no notice of the second line and walked straight in.

"What kept ya?"

McGurk looked angry. His red hair seemed redder—almost as inflamed as the rabbits' noses—and his green eyes were flashing. He was sitting on his chair at the head of the long table and rocking rapidly with impatience.

"Sorry!" I said. "But—hey! What's this? Easter treats for the staff?"

I was looking at the box on the table in front of McGurk. The box was made of cardboard, but it wasn't any of those we use for filing clues or records of our cases in. It was smaller. A shoe box. But it was crammed full of goodies: brightly colored packs and tubes and cans of candy.

"Don't touch!" said McGurk, slapping Willie's hand as it reached toward a can of Sour Hard Candy Drops—his favorites. "These aren't for us. They're for official business."

By now I had forgotten all about the rabbits.

"Official business?" I said.

"Yeah!" growled McGurk. "That's what I called this meeting for. A new idea I've had. And since Wanda doesn't seem to be able to make it this morning, we'll go right ahead without her."

"But—what's official business got to do with"— Willie stared hungrily at the can, then gulped—"Sour Hard Candy Drops?"

McGurk sat back. He'd stopped rocking. He was smirking. He loves to keep us guessing—the jerk.

"To pay for information with," he said.

"Pay who?" said Willie. "What information? I can tell you all sorts of stuff about Seattle, where I was born. And—and about making paper, which my father sells. And—and—no?"

"No, Willie." McGurk was shaking his head slowly, still smirking. "I don't mean that sort of information. I mean—"

"Information about *crimes!*" I said, suddenly getting it. "Right, McGurk?"

"Right!" he grunted. He was a bit miffed at not keeping *me* guessing. "But since it's my idea, maybe you'll let me finish explaining. O.K.?"

"Go ahead, go ahead," I mumbled.

"Thank you. . . . Yes, Willie. I've decided that the McGurk Organization should use a method that all police everywhere use, when they're stuck for vital information. And that is to have a network of informers. Snitches. Know what I mean?"

Willie's eyes had widened.

"Gee! Yeah! Like those guys the detectives go to meet on television. In railroad stations, and old back lots, and dark dead-end streets late at night. And they don't look at each other when they talk, and they talk out of the side of their mouths, because it's got to be kept secret, yeah. Because if it isn't kept secret, the guys the informer talks about will know who snitched on them and—and. . . ."

Willie gave up there, and no wonder. It was one of the longest speeches he'd made in his life, maybe a record.

"You've got it, Willie."

"And—and"—Willie was starting up again—"the cop gives the snitch a few dollars, and the snitch is always wanting more. But the cop has to be careful, because the police department don't have all that much money to spare and—and—gee!"

"Right again, Willie!" said McGurk. "And that's going to be the way it is with us, too. Even though we'll be trading candy instead of cash. In fact," he said, reaching for a sheet of paper from under the shoe box, "I've already made out a scale of payments. I want you to type it out, Joey, and make five

copies. One for the bulletin board and one for each
of us."

I stared at the list, and here it is, typed:

Scale of Pay for Informers

A. For a small clue about a crime being
   investigated:
   10 chocolate-covered peanuts, OR
   5 Sour Hard Candy Drops, OR
   5 Pop Drops

B. For a good clue about a crime being
   investigated:
   6 Cherry Chiclets, OR
   12 licorice candies

C. For a rumor about a crime being planned:
   6 Sweetarts, OR
   1 Twizzler strip

D. For a definite first-hand tip-off about
   a crime being planned:
   1 pack chocolate-covered peanuts, OR
   1 pack licorice candy, OR
   1 pack Chuckles

E. For information leading straight to
   arrest of criminal:
   1 pack Twizzlers, OR
   1 Marathon bar, OR
   2 almond-flavored coconut bars

N.B. There is NO payment for information
   given BY officers of the McGurk
   Organization

McGurk looked up when he saw that I'd finished reading the list. He was smiling happily.

"So all we need now is a case to work on."

Willie nodded. He'd been very busy reading the list, but now he was all alert.

"Hey! Yeah! Well! I think we've got one. Somebody's been going around painting the rabbits. Do I get to have five Sour Hard Candy Drops for that information?"

McGurk slapped his hand before it could reach the can. I tapped the list.

"Read the bottom line, Willie, the bottom line. The scale doesn't apply to us. Anyway," I continued, looking at McGurk, "it seems more of a joke than a crime."

McGurk frowned.

"You mean the paint on the rabbits?"

"Yes. It—"

"Huh!" he grunted. "Some joke! Vandalism is more like it. I mean I *liked* my rabbit the way it was. It looks stupid now. I mean if I wanted it painted I'd have painted it myself."

"So you think it does rate as a crime?" I said. "A case?"

His freckles bunched together as he wrinkled his nose.

"No. Not really. Just a bit of dumb fooling. Besides, it's *obvious* who did it."

"Eh?" said Willie, looking up from the list with a start.

"Yeah!" said McGurk. "Fooling around with lawn ornaments. It's got the same M.O. all over it."

"M.O.?" said Willie. "Is that the shade of paint?"

"No," I said. "It means Method of Operation." I turned to McGurk. I suddenly realized what he meant: something that had happened about two years ago. "You mean you think it was—?"

Just then Wanda entered, all breathless.

"Yes," said McGurk, not even glancing at her. "I think it's obvious who did it. Wanda and her brother."

2 Wanda Is Worried

I don't think Wanda knew what we were talking about at first. I don't think she even heard what McGurk had said. Apart from being breathless, she looked as if she had problems of her own.

"Have—have you seen what—what's happened—to—to the rabbits?" she said, leaning on the table and trying to get her breath back.

"Yes," said McGurk. "And I don't think it's very funny."

She stared at him, frowning. She didn't even glance at the box of candy in front of him. Then I was sure she was very worried.

"Well I don't think it's very funny either!" she said. "Especially when the wrong people get blamed!"

McGurk just sneered—and boy, how he can sneer when he wants! Wanda began to flush with anger. I stepped back. Only Willie seemed puzzled.

"Who, Wanda? Who's getting blamed?"

"I am," she said. "And my brother."

"Your brother Ed?" asked Willie, his voice full of awe.

That is the way most kids speak about Ed Grieg around here. He is only seventeen, but he's over six feet tall already. His hair is a kind of dull blond, like Wanda's, and he wears it nearly as long. During the last summer vacation he grew a gunfighter mustache, a beauty. My father would like to grow one as thick. But what makes him a hero with us kids is the fact that he is the best swimmer at the high school, the best long-distance runner, the regular quarterback for the school football team, and the number-one baseball pitcher. And if you're like me and respect brains as well as muscle—well, he's got them too. He never gets anything less than straight A's for math and science. No wonder they call him Grieg the Greatest.

Wanda wasn't looking so proud, though, as she turned to Willie. Just sour.

"Yes. My brother Ed. What other brother do I have?"

Then she turned back to McGurk.

"And we're innocent!"

McGurk's sneer turned into a laugh. A slow jeering laugh.

"Har! *har!*" he said.

"But we are!" cried Wanda, banging the table and making the candy bounce and rustle in its box.

McGurk stood up and leaned over. His eyes were slitty gleams.

"All right, then," he said. "So let's see your hands. Right now."

Without even pausing to think, Wanda held out her hands, palms up.

McGurk pounced.

"There!" he yelled, stabbing a finger at one of Wanda's. "What's *that* then?"

We others stared. Wanda frowned.

"Well—it's—I guess it's—"

"Red paint!" said McGurk, still stabbing at the smear on Wanda's right index finger. "Exactly the same shade!"

"Well sure!" yelled Wanda. She looked mad again, curling up her right hand more to make a fist than to hide the smear. "But it's only because I touched our rabbit's ears to see if it really *was* paint."

Willie spoke up. He'd been looking at his own hand.

"Yeah!" he said. "Me too. Look. That's how I got mine, under this nail here, where I scratched at the paint. And *I* didn't do it!"

"Me either!" I said, surprised to find that even I had a faint trace of the paint from touching the second rabbit. Then I noticed a sudden movement of McGurk's. Nothing very startling. Just a quick closing up of his own hands and putting them out of sight under the table. "All right, McGurk!" I said. "Why don't you show us *your* fingers?"

He glared at me for a second or two, then shrugged.

"So what?" he said. "So I touched the paint too. But that isn't what makes me suspect you and Ed, Wanda. And you *know* it!"

Wanda just groaned. I was nodding, agreeing with

McGurk this time. Again Willie looked puzzled.

"*I* don't know it," he said. "Why *should* you suspect them?"

Wanda sighed.

"It's the same old story, Willie. You do something wrong just once, and everyone blames you if something like it ever happens again. . . . All the dumbbells do, anyway!" she added, giving me and Mc-Gurk a glare.

"What—what was this thing you and Ed did then?" asked Willie, looking as if he expected it to be First Degree Murder at least.

"It's what I was saying about the M.O.," explained McGurk. "It was another case where lawn ornaments were fooled around with."

But even he had to grin as he remembered it.

"Yes, except—" began Wanda.

"The Great Elfweight Championship of the World," I said, remembering the banner in the front yard of the house opposite the Griegs.

"The Great *what?*" asked Willie.

Then we told him.

The people who lived opposite the Griegs at that time were called Madison. One day they bought a whole bunch of garden gnomes and stuck them around in the yard. There were gnomes fishing, and gnomes chasing butterflies, and gnomes waving, and gnomes sleeping, and gnomes just sitting.

"Some of the neighbors thought they looked great and some thought they looked awful," said Wanda. "I could take them or leave them, but Ed was very scornful. 'I think gnomes in a yard are bad news!' he said. 'Or as Dad would say: *definitely square.*' Then I thought of a joke."

Wanda smiled as she recalled it.

"I was only eight at the time—this was all of two years ago—but I had this flash of wit. I said, 'Sure it's square, Ed. It's the Madisons', isn't it? The Madisons' Square Garden.' "

I laughed.

"That was quite good for a kid of eight, Wanda," I said.

"Never mind the compliments," said McGurk. "Tell Willie what happened next."

"Well, that gave Ed the idea," she said. " 'Madison Square Garden,' he said. 'Sure! Where all the big fights are held in New York. And that's just what we'll stage in the Madison yard. The Elfweight Championship of the World.' "

I'll never forget it, myself. It took place on the Memorial Day weekend. The Madisons left on Friday for a trip to the Catskills, and on Saturday morning there it was, all laid out on their front yard.

The centerpiece was a model boxing ring.

Inside it were three gnomes. Two of them had the cutest little leather boxing gloves and real silk boxer shorts. One was stretched out on the canvas. He was one of the sleeping gnomes, but the way he was dressed it looked just as if he'd been knocked out. The other gnome boxer was one of those that are made to look as if they're jumping up in surprise, both arms in the air. But with the gloves on he looked like all boxers do when they're triumphant. And the third gnome in the ring was one of the waving gnomes. But the arm he held in the air was now touching one of the winner's upraised arms, so that he looked just like a referee declaring the result.

"And that wasn't all," said McGurk, getting all warmed up at the memory. "There were spectator gnomes on little wood benches all around the ring. You know—some of them with their arms in the air like they were cheering. Heh! heh!"

"But the one I liked the best," I said, "was the one selling popcorn."

"You're kidding!" said Willie.

His eyes were shining, yet he looked wistful too—

sad to think he'd been thousands of miles away when all this took place.

"No," I said. "This was a gnome carrying a flower pot. But this time it had been filled with popcorn instead of flowers. And there he was, standing among the spectator gnomes."

"People came from all over town to see it," said McGurk.

"There was even a small crowd on Monday, when the Madisons got back," said Wanda.

"What did they say?" asked Willie.

"Well," said Wanda, "they were a bit shook up at first. Then miffed. But even they had to laugh in the end. After we'd cleared it all up and put the gnomes back in their proper places."

"Gee!" said Willie. "That must have been some sight, Wanda! But—hee! hee!—I gotta hand it to you. This rabbit stunt wasn't bad either. I nearly laughed myself sick this morning."

Wanda rolled her eyes and groaned.

"You too!" Then she turned to McGurk and me. "Listen!" she said. "We *did not* do it! This—this stupid rabbit painting isn't in the same *class* as the gnome stunt."

I looked at McGurk and he looked at me. We

nodded. Now that we'd had our memory refreshed, it did seem that Wanda had a point there.

"What's more," said Wanda, "childish though it is, we've just got to find the real painter."

"Oh?" said McGurk. "Why?"

"Because Ed and I are going to have our allowances stopped for a month if we don't. Our parents think we did it, too."

"Tough!" murmured McGurk. His eyes were slitty, but I could tell he still wasn't quite sure of Wanda's innocence. After all, the rabbit stunt wasn't all that bad. "But what—"

"Anyway," said Wanda, giving the table another bang and tossing the hair out of her face scornfully, "if you won't believe *me*, maybe you'll believe Ed. He's on his way. He wants to hire us to find the real perpetrators."

That made McGurk rock back in his chair.

"On his way *here?* Ed? Ed Grieg? Your *brother* Ed?"

Wanda nodded.

McGurk jumped to his feet.

"Well why didn't you say so before? Willie, stand by the door, ready to let him in immediately. You others, help me tidy up the desk. Come on! Move it!"

We moved.

We'd had all sorts of people visit the office, adults as well as children. We'd even had a real policeman once.

But Grieg the Greatest was something else.

"Listen!" said Willie. "I think I hear him now!"

3 Grieg the Greatest

You know, I'm not so sure I'm all that crazy about super heroes, after all. They're great from a distance, when you're in the crowd and they're down there on the field, pitching their curve balls or making brilliant passes. But up close, in everyday life, they can be pretty hard to take.

Like Ed Grieg that morning.

I mean here was a guy who never even *looked* at us kids in the street, even though his sister was a good friend of ours. But now he was in trouble, needing our help. So how did he act?

Politely?

Well, of course, we didn't really expect him to call

any of us "sir" or grovel or anything, anyway.

Pleasantly?

We didn't expect him to be a million laughs, either, the trouble he was in.

But that guy didn't even knock on the door.

And he didn't even smile—not once.

He just slammed straight in, nearly busting Willie's nose with the swing of the door. Then he marched straight across the room (it only took him three strides), straight past McGurk (standing there with his hand out in welcome), and straight to McGurk's chair. I guess if McGurk had been sitting in it, Ed would have hauled him right out. As it was, he ignored McGurk's hand completely and sat down, rocking like *he* was the Head of the Organization.

Then he spoke.

"I guess she's told you why I'm here?"

He didn't even glance at the "she" he'd mentioned —his own sister.

He did glance at the candy, however. And in glancing at it he must have decided it was an Easter treat for anyone who stopped by. He grabbed a double pack of coconut bars and started to peel it.

"Yes, Ed," murmured McGurk, still starry-eyed. "And you sure came to the right—"

"Yeah! yeah!" said the big hero, taking a bite that

was worth at least one tip-off about a crime not yet committed. "Save the sales pitch, kid. I'm only hiring you because it takes kids to catch kids in a fool kid thing like this rabbit caper."

"Yes, well," said McGurk, not looking quite so pleased. "We do have a pretty good record. We—"

Ed finished his first coconut bar and interrupted McGurk again.

"Talking about records, I brought this."

He reached into his windbreaker and pulled out a notebook. It was the big hard-backed school kind.

"Oh?" I said. I keep all our records, so naturally I was interested in this. "What is it a record of?"

He ignored me. He opened the book and started on the second coconut bar.

"First," he said, looking at McGurk, "I guess she told you how I had nothing to do with those rabbits?"

"Well, sure!" said McGurk. "Sure thing, Ed! I mean it's a laugh, blaming *you* for a thing like *that*. We know *you* wouldn't have done it."

"Humph!" went Wanda. "It's different *now*, isn't it? It—"

But Ed interrupted his sister. Even her, Wanda, his codefendant.

He gave McGurk a hard look.

"So you think I'm innocent, huh? Just on my say-so? What kind of a detective *are* you, anyway? Taking someone's *word* for it?"

"Well, I—I mean—I—"

"I don't have an alibi. I can't prove I was miles away last night or early this morning, when it must have happened. I've even gotten some of the paint on my fingers." Ed held up a hand. The fingers were huge, like a bunch of sausages. And there was a smear of red on them. And chocolate, too.

He licked off the chocolate.

"But I think this should convince you," he said, tapping the book. "Solid proof. It shows the way I work. When Ed Grieg plans a stunt he really plans it. Look."

It was open at the first page. I got Wanda to borrow the book later, and we took it along to the library and had a photocopy made of that page, just for the record. This is it:

The Madison Square Garden Project

Supervisor: E. J. Grieg
Assistant: W. Grieg
Purpose: To arrange the gnomes in the
    Madisons' front yard like a
    world champion. fight.
First calculations: The average height of
    the gnomes is 1 ft. 6 in. Therefore
    they are approximately 1/4 the size
    of human beings. Therefore every-
    thing in the set up must be
    1/4 the size of actual items.

    E.g. (a) the size of the ring;
        (b) the height of the ropes;
        (c) the distance between ropes;
        (d) the height of the corner
            posts and stools, etc.;
        (e) the size of the towels and
            pails carried by the "boxers"
            handlers.

And so it went on—pages and pages and pages like that. Calculations, drawings, plans—all connected with the Great Elfweight Championship of the World. Why, there were even pages for Wanda to work from: like with boxing glove patterns and suggestions for using scraps of leather from an old armchair.

We were really impressed. I myself was so impressed that I forgave Ed all his obnoxious behavior and he became my Number One Hero again, right there and then.

"So now you've seen some actual evidence," he said, looking around at us. "So do you believe that anyone who can plan like this—even two years ago, even as a mere child of fifteen—would *stoop* to a lousy stunt like daubing up those dumb rabbits?"

"No!" we all said—McGurk, Willie, and me. "No way! Never!"

"Right," said Grieg the Greatest. "Now I'm not saying Wanda here wouldn't do it, on her own, without my help. But I'm clean on this one and I want you to prove it the only way our mother and father will accept. By catching the creep who did it. And fast. O.K.?"

Then he picked up a Marathon bar and strutted out the way he'd strutted in.

"Don't worry, Ed!" McGurk sang out after him. "We won't let you down!"

"You bet!" said Willie.

"We'll give it our very best shots!" I said.

But all Wanda did was murmur "Hmm!" in a very gruff way.

I guess she hadn't liked what Ed had said about *her* being capable of "stooping to daub dumb rabbits."

I guess she was thinking that being the sister of a Super Hero is all very good, but it can be pretty tough at times.

Then she snapped out of it when McGurk took charge again. Nothing Ed had done or said had discouraged *him*. Instead, McGurk seemed determined to show that he could be just as thorough as any old Ed Grieg.

"Right, men. We'll take the case. And first we go right to where it all began. See if we can pick up any leads there."

"Where's that?" asked Willie.

"The Rabbit Factory itself," said McGurk. "Donny Towers' place. You never know. He might even have decided to go around putting spots of color on the rabbits himself. So they'd stand out better and his helpers wouldn't go trying to sell them at the same house twice."

◢4 The Rabbit Factory

Donny's place was a hive of activity when we got there. Or maybe I should say a *warren* of activity, because these were rabbits he was dealing in, not bees.

The first sign was his old Chevy, out on the street.

"That means they're still busy," said McGurk. "Donny's been using his garage exclusively for rabbit production for the past two weeks."

"Yes. And using his yard as a showcase," said Wanda.

She pointed to the three rabbits out on the front lawn. These were samples of the three basic types that Donny had been making. There was a sitting-up rabbit, like the kind in my yard. There was a crouching, nibbling rabbit, like the one in Willie's yard. And there was a rabbit running with its ears back—the kind chosen by Mrs. McGurk.

"Hey, look!" said Willie. "*They've* been painted, too!"

He was right.

The sitting-up rabbit had a red nose.

The crouching rabbit had a pair of red ears.

And the running rabbit had a red tail and four red feet.

"It looks like the Mystery Painter decided to give samples of *his* basic styles," I said.

"Yeah!" McGurk grunted. "So let's find out what Donny can tell us."

The garage doors were wide open and we could see that McGurk's description had been pretty good. It really was a rabbit factory. The whole of one side was taken up by a long workbench—two picnic tables placed end to end—and it was crowded with rabbits of all three kinds. Rabbits and parts of rabbits.

Donny saw us.

"Hi, there!" he called out, looking up from the bench. "Come right on in. You want to buy some more Easter bunnies?"

Donny is a big guy. He has a bushy black beard

and he looks like a wrestler, a real gorilla. But he is really very gentle.

As we went in, he combed his fingers through the beard. It's a habit he's got. But because his hands were all sticky with the light-gray goo, it had made his beard look funny. It looked as if he'd started to go gray himself. What added to this impression was the worried look on his face, which he kept trying to erase with a grin. It made it seem like he'd gone gray with worry.

"No, Donny," said McGurk. Then he remembered to be official. "We're here on business, Mr. Towers. We're inquiring about the red paint."

"Oh, that!" said Donny, with a shrug. "Well, I can't help you there, I'm afraid. It's just as big a mystery to us. But come in, anyway."

There were three other people in there with him. There was Joanne Cooper, his girl friend, and two helpers called Sam and Ferdie, each about nineteen or twenty. Joanne lived next door to the Griegs and was quite friendly with Wanda. But like her boy friend, she too looked rather sad as she said: "Hi, Wanda! Nice of you to stop by."

"I was just thinking that it might have been *you* who had done all the painting," said McGurk, giving Donny one of his hard green stares.

If he'd been expecting Donny to blush behind his beard, McGurk was disappointed.

The social worker didn't even blink.

"Why should I want to do a thing like that?" he asked, but without much interest.

McGurk told him his theory. Donny shook his head.

"We don't really need to *see* the rabbits to remind us who bought them," he said. "We have a list."

McGurk still kept up his hard look.

"You don't seem very worried about the painting, Mr. Towers."

"Why should I be?" said Donny. "They're not great works of art, after all."

"You can say that again!" said Sam, laughing.

"In fact *I* think they been *improved!*" said Ferdie, also laughing.

The two helpers were much more cheerful than Donny and Joanne, I noticed. But I didn't think much of it right then. I could see we were wasting our time, so I turned to McGurk and said:

"Well, don't you think we'd better go and—?"

He gave me a frown and shook his head to shut me up. I wondered what he was up to.

Maybe he'd spotted something I hadn't.

But all he did was turn back to Donny and say: "Can we see how the rabbits are made, Mr. Towers?"

This made me really suspicious. I knew for a fact that McGurk wasn't usually interested in how things are made. Especially when he's on a case. So why now?

And then, as he moved over to the bench next to Sam, it suddenly hit me.

Of course!

This was his great chance.

You see, there was a rumor going around the neighborhood that Donny's two most recent helpers were ex-convicts. The word was that Sam had been a pickpocket and Ferdie a car thief.

So this was McGurk's great chance to study the criminal mind at close range. If only a *reformed* criminal mind.

I took a deep breath as I glanced at the two cheerful but very tough-looking guys. I sure hoped McGurk would be tactful about it!

Anyway, Donny said he'd be delighted to show us the works and we all crowded around the bench and at first everything went fine.

I was genuinely interested in how the rabbits were made, and I think Willie was, too.

"It's a kind of mass-production method," said Donny. "We each make separate parts and then put them together. The raw material is over there."

He pointed to a big tank opposite the bench, over by the far wall. It was partly full of water, and in the water was a big sack of clay.

"The water keeps the clay nice and soft," said Donny. "Otherwise it would set hard before we used it."

"You said something about each person making separate parts," I said.

"Right," said Donny. "I make the heads and tails."

"And I make the legs," said Sam.

"I'm the ears man," said Ferdie.

"And I make the bodies," said Joanne.

"So what we do is take a hunk of clay from the sack and make enough parts for four or five rabbits at a time," said Donny. "According to the pattern on the wall there."

This was nailed above the workbench, and because it became very important to us later in the case, I have made a copy on the same kind of graph paper for the records:

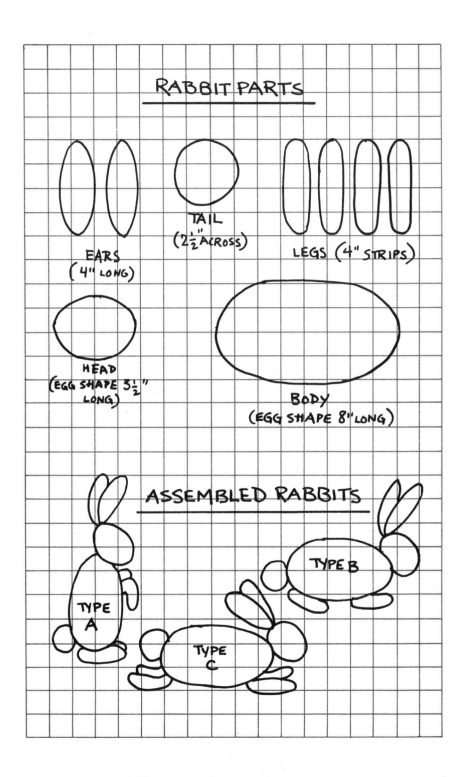

RABBIT PARTS

EARS
(4" LONG)

TAIL
(2½" ACROSS)

LEGS (4" STRIPS)

HEAD
(EGG SHAPE 3½" LONG)

BODY
(EGG SHAPE 8" LONG)

ASSEMBLED RABBITS

TYPE A

TYPE B

TYPE C

"The trick when assembling them is to make sure the clay is sticky enough to hold the parts together until it all sets."

"You can say that again, man!" said Ferdie.

"The first batch we made all shook loose as soon as we took them out to the car," said Joanne.

"There was bits and pieces all over," said Sam, pointing to a small heap in the far corner of the garage, with rabbit ears and tails and legs sticking out.

"That's the reject pile," said Donny.

Well, as I mentioned, Willie and I were finding this all very interesting. But the others—no. I could see that McGurk was looking at Sam and Ferdie as if he was dying to question them about their life of crime. And after a while I could see something else: the way Wanda kept staring at Joanne's hands.

Joanne's fingers were all gooey with the clay, too, but I thought Wanda may have spotted some red paint on them or something.

But it wasn't that at all.

"Joanne, why aren't you wearing your engagement ring?" she said.

Joanne and Donny had become officially engaged about a month ago. I'd forgotten all about it. Trust Wanda to remember a thing like that, though!

Joanne sort of laughed.

"Honey! I'd *ruin* it, dabbling in all this clay."

"I guess so," said Wanda. "But may I see it again? It's a beautiful ring."

She looked around on the bench, near Joanne's pocketbook, expecting to see it in a safe place there.

"It—I—" began Joanne.

Then Donny broke in.

"It's gone for alteration. It—it didn't fit. Too small."

Wanda frowned.

"But it looked all right the other day. You were wearing it then."

Joanne gave Donny an impatient look.

"No, no! Donny's got it wrong. It was too *big*. It's gone to be tightened."

I could see that for some reason they were both very embarrassed. I thought maybe they'd had a fight or something, and Joanne had given Donny the ring back, and he was trying to persuade her to accept it again. Still and all, they *looked* friendly enough.

Anyway, that wasn't the only embarrassing moment, because just then McGurk's restraint gave way.

Still staring at Sam with glowing eyes, he said:

"Hey, Sam, is it true you used to be a pick—"

"*McGurk!*" cried Wanda.

She looked as shocked as I felt. Even Willie had started to blush.

But Sam only laughed.

"That's O.K.," he said to Wanda. "So long as he says *used to be,* I don't mind a bit." He turned to McGurk. "You were gonna say did I used to be a pickpocket, right?"

Now McGurk himself was blushing.

"Well—no. I'm sorry! You—I guess you don't look the type—I mean—"

Again Sam laughed.

"No? Well sure enough, I never do it for real,

these days. Only at parties, for laughs. But I *was* a professional. One of the best. Right, Ferdie?"

Ferdie grinned.

"*The* best, man! Used to call him Super Dip, around Times Square."

"And just to prove it, here's my pickpocket's ID," said Sam, digging into his back pocket.

McGurk began to laugh.

"Come *on!* Pickpockets don't have—"

Then he gaped.

For it *was* an ID card that Sam had drawn out of his pocket. A very familiar ID card. With the words *The McGurk Organization* on the front. One of those I'd typed myself—one for each member. *In fact it was McGurk's own!*

"Hey!"

McGurk yelped as he shot a hand into his pocket. Then he took it out, empty, and went on staring at Sam in astonishment.

Everyone laughed, except McGurk. Even Donny and Joanne seemed to forget their worries for a moment.

Then McGurk rounded on us.

"You," he said, scowling at me, "get busy! We're here on an investigation. You should be making notes." He tapped my notebook, which I'd placed on the bench. "Put down that Donny and Joanne have no idea who did the painting. Or Sam and Ferdie. That right?"

He looked around at them. All four shook their heads.

"Go *on* then!". said McGurk, to me. "Get it down."

But this was where the third embarrassing thing happened. I couldn't find my pencil.

"I put it down here, next to the book," I said. "It was only a short stub of a pencil, but—"

"Maybe it rolled under one of the rabbit parts here," said Wanda, lifting up one of the big egg shapes that Joanne had made for a body.

"Or on the floor," said Willie, bending down.

"Or in someone's *pocket!*" said McGurk, suddenly leering at Sam.

Sam shook his head.

"Not this time. Not me. Honest."

"Well where—?"

"Hold it!"

Willie's voice came from down among our legs. He was staring up at Wanda.

"Hold what?" she said. "This lump of clay?"

She said it in a smart-aleck sort of way, but Willie nodded rapidly, his face serious.

"Yes," he said. "Just hold it up higher and *you'll* see it, too."

And she did. And there was the pencil stuck in the bottom of the lump of clay.

Suddenly Donny became very brisk. He started tugging at his beard and looking at his watch.

"Look, guys," he said, "we're going to have to break for lunch soon and we *are* kind of busy."

"Right! right!" said Joanne, suddenly very brisk herself.

"So if there's anything else you'd like to know," said Donny, "hurry it up, please."

Well I guess there was plenty McGurk would have liked to learn from Sam and Ferdie about the methods of pickpockets and car thieves. But it wasn't strictly business, and even he could take a hint.

"No. That's about it," he said. "Thank you for your time." Then, trying to look very important and make up for the ribbing he'd had over the ID card, he said in his best Police Lieutenant voice: "We have work to do, too, men. I want us to see what the word is out on the streets. Check with all our informers."

As we left the garage, I happened to look back. Donny and Joanne had gone off into a far corner, but Sam and Ferdie were holding on to each other's shoulders, shaking. I could tell they were trying desperately not to laugh out loud.

McGurk had impressed *them* all right!

5 The Owl

I once read this in a book:

"Detectives are only as good as their informers."

I also read this in another book:

"Most crimes are solved as a result of tip-offs."

I can now state that all of that is true.

Before, when we'd tried real police methods, we'd had all kinds of problems. Like when we gathered clues from a particular area. Or when we shadowed people. Or when we questioned suspects. These activities are a whole lot easier when you read about them than when you actually *do* them.

But using informers is a breeze. Especially when the word gets around that you have something to pay them with.

At 11:30 that morning, right after visiting the Rabbit Factory, we hit the streets. Each of us had a pocketful of assorted candy and an earful of warnings from McGurk.

"Make sure you don't eat the informers' payroll yourselves!" he kept saying fiercely.

By 12:30 we had paid out:

most of the chocolate-covered peanuts;

all the Pop Drops;

about half of the Sour Hard Candy Drops;

most of the licorice candies;

2 packs Cherry Chiclets;

3 Twizzler strips; and

1 Marathon bar.

But by then we had also gotten the names of the Mystery Painter and his gang.

There was no mistake. When we compared notes after lunch we found that nearly every informer had fingered the same guys. Mind you, the fact that the leader of the gang had one of the biggest mouths in town helped some. In fact Brains Bellingham was right in what he told me. If we'd simply hung around and kept our ears open, we'd probably have heard the bragging of the Mystery Painter ourselves, without having to give away all that candy.

Anyway, here's a sample of how easy it was. This

is the record of my interview with little Brains Bellingham. He's only nine but I guess he must have an I.Q. of 900. I found him in the library—naturally.

Brains has fair hair, which he wears short and bristly. He once told me it helped him to think better. He said too much hair draws energy away from the brain. He might have been kidding—you can never tell with him. He is only a shrimp of a kid but he has bigger glasses than mine and they give him an owlish look. But don't ever be fooled by that. Owls are very quick to pounce on tidbits, remember.

"Hi, Brains!"

He looked up from the book he was glancing through, over by the Science and Engineering stack. He blinked.

"Oh, hi, Joey! . . . Hey! I bet even *you* don't know what 'thermonuclear' means, do you? I do."

(All these *doo-yoo-I-doo* noises made him really *sound* like an owl.)

"Forget that," I said. "I'm looking for information."

"Well this is the place for it."

"I don't mean *book* information. I mean *street* information."

"They keep the Town Guide over at the desk."

"I don't mean *that* kind of street information. I mean information about a crime."

He looked at me sideways.

"Ah-*hah!* I get you. You're on detective business, right? For the McGurk Organization, right? You know, Joey, I never could understand how a bright guy like you could team up with that dumb McGurk. Especially when you could be helping me to build a computer or something. But go on—what crime?"

"The rabbits."

"Oo-oo-oh!" (Again like an owl, low and flute-like.) "That one." He suddenly started acting like all the snitches I'd ever seen on TV. He hunched over his book and turned away. "You do the same, man," he muttered, just loud enough for me to hear. "Pretend to be reading. I think I might have something for you."

"Great!" I muttered, opening up a copy of *Science for Fun* and peering into it. "Shoot!"

"Uh!" He turned slightly, his face still hidden behind the covers of *Adventures with the Atom.* "What's it worth?"

"Depends," I muttered.

"On what?" he murmured.

"On how good the information is. Listen."

I put the scale-of-payments list inside my book and read it out.

"Dumb!" he murmured into his *Adventures with the Atom*.

"Why?" I asked my *Science for Fun*.

"How can you tell a *small* clue isn't a *good* clue until you've followed it up? Or whether it won't lead straight to an arrest, for that matter?"

He had a point, but I wasn't there to argue.

"Well forget that for now. What's your information?"

"It'll cost you top rates. A whole Marathon bar."

"We'll see," I said.

"We'll see no deal then. So long!"

He began to drift away.

"No! Wait!" I said. "O.K. A whole bar—but only half now. Then I'll see what I think when you've told me."

"Deal. Give. Slide the half bar into that space on the shelf. Between *Man's Conquest of the Stars* and *Ocean Explorers*."

I did that. Then he moved over and slid it out and into his pocket—as neatly as Sam the Super Dip in reverse.

"All right," he said. "Promise you won't tell who told you?"

"Promise," I said.

"I mean this could get me into trouble with the Mob."

"Look!" I said. "Quit playing games! Do you have a name or don't you?"

"O.K., then. I won't say it out loud. The place might be bugged. But just follow my finger while I spell it out."

I looked over his shoulder and watched as he

point to a *b*, then a *u*, then an *r*, then a *t*. By then I had it—*Burt Rafferty*—but I let Brains finish, just to make him work for his candy.

"Him!" I said.

"Yes. Him. And his mob. Do I get the other half now?"

"You sure about this?"

"Positive."

"Here you are, then."

It figured somehow. It was just the sort of trick Burt Rafferty and his buddies would pull. But I still wasn't satisfied that Brains hadn't just guessed it.

"How do you know?"

"I thought I heard them. Just after eight last night. Just after dark. I was looking down from my bedroom window." (Again the owl!) "So when I saw the paint on the rabbits this morning, I did a little investigating on my own."

"Oh?"

"Sure. The McGurk Organization doesn't have *exclusive* detection rights in this neighborhood, you know."

"Go on. What sort of investigation did you do?"

"Real scientific investigation. None of this kid stuff. I scraped a sample of paint off my rabbit's nose and placed it carefully in an envelope. Then I took a walk around to Burt Rafferty's house."

"Why go there?"

"Because I keep my eyes open. And because he'd tried to sell me an old bike of his only last week."

"What has that got to do with it?"

"He'd given it a new coat of paint. Red. A bright orange-red."

"Oh, you mean—?"

"Yes. I matched it against the sample. Same shade exactly." Brains laughed. "Besides—heh! heh!—Burt didn't even bother to deny it. He's going around shooting his mouth off about painting the rabbits. Thinks it was a terrific idea. You'd have heard sooner or later, without handing out candy." He bit into his. "Dumb!" he mumbled.

"Don't speak with your mouth full!" I muttered.

But he was right. Absolutely right. That was the name all the others came back with, too. McGurk had gotten it from five different people and it had only cost him half a pack of chocolate-covered peanuts and five Pop Drops. Wanda had paid out even less for her information. Only Willie had been more generous than me. (But there was a suspicious smear of chocolate in the corner of his mouth and his breath *reeked* of licorice.)

"So now we grill Rafferty until he breaks!" said McGurk, grimly. "Let's go, men!"

Well, I won't bother you with much of that. Rafferty needed no grilling. Again Brains had been right. Burt was boasting even before we'd reached him.

"Hi, guys! Some stunt we pulled last night, huh? Everybody's laughing about it!"

"Yeah!" said Wanda, dryly. "You should hear my folks. Killing themselves!"

McGurk himself was a bit miffed at getting a confession so easily. He even pretended not to believe Burt.

"Come off it! You haven't the nerve! Or the brains!"

"Oh, no, McJerk? Well you're just jealous, that's all!"

"Prove you did it then!" sneered McGurk.

And darn it if Burt didn't do just that. He showed us the empty can of paint and the brush they'd used on some rabbits, and a spray can they'd used on others when the first can had run out. He told us

where the two different types had been used, and sure enough it checked out. He even mentioned spilling some drops on the Griegs' front lawn and that checked out, too.

"So you see," said Burt, grinning. "I *did* do it. Me and the guys. As soon as I saw those Easter bunnies appear on the lawns last week, I got the idea. The greatest stunt since the gnomes in the Madison yard that time!"

"Baloney!" said McGurk. "This was just a crummy carbon copy. Kid stuff."

"And those gnomes weren't damaged in any way," I said. "They didn't get all daubed up."

"Who's worried?" said Burt. "It'll rub off with paint remover."

"*I'm* worried, for one!" said Wanda. We were still standing on her front lawn and she glanced unhappily at the house. "They think I had something to do with it and they've stopped my allowance."

"Now isn't that just too bad!" jeered Burt. Then his grin spread fat and wide, and his eyes lit up. "Hey! Wait till I tell the others! It makes it an even bigger laugh!"

"*Oh, yeah?*" growled a voice behind him. What looked like a pound of muscular sausages dropped heavily on his shoulder and jerked him around. "Well

I don't think so, sonny, because *my* allowance has been stopped too!"

It was Grieg the Greatest himself. And of course that was *that*. Burt couldn't wait to go and confess to Mrs. Grieg and convince her the way he'd convinced us.

As Wanda said later:

"It isn't as if he was just *afraid* of Ed. But my brother is such a big hero that Burt would have owned up to it even if he hadn't done it. Just for the honor! *Wanda* Grieg gets into trouble and it's all a big laugh. But to oblige *Ed* Grieg, anything!"

She sounded bitter. In fact we all felt a bit low. The whole thing had been too easy—and it had cost us a lot of candy.

But we needn't have felt that way. The rabbit case was warming up, not winding up. Because you know what? Inside the next twelve hours they all disappeared. Overnight. Just as if they'd run off in the moonlight. Every rabbit in every yard: the red-eared, the red-eyed, the red-tailed, and the red-nosed, along with all those that hadn't been touched by spray or brush.

6 The Three Prime Suspects

This time we had nothing to go on. No eyewitnesses. No bragging. No rumors.

The Great Rabbit Rip-Off had taken place in the early hours of the morning and the only clues we had at first concerned the time.

Willie provided one of those clues.

"My mother and father had been out at a party. When they got back at one o'clock the rabbits were still there."

The Sandowskys' car headlights had lit up the two rabbits on our front lawn, and Mr. Sandowsky had nearly tripped over their rabbit, which Willie had put on the porch near the door.

The other clue about the time was given by Simon

Emmet. He's a newsboy and he delivers early. By the time he was on his route, the rabbits had all disappeared.

"So that puts it somewhere between one and seven," said McGurk, that Saturday morning, as we gathered in his basement to discuss the news. He looked up and stopped rocking. "Where was Ed during that time, Wanda?"

"At home, of course. Why?"

"You sure?"

"Well as far as I know, yes. He was in bed like the rest of us. I mean *he* wasn't out at a party or anything. He's in training for baseball and he's very particular about getting nine hours' sleep every night. But why?"

"Because," said McGurk, still looking slitty and doubtful, "it would be just the sort of stunt he'd pull."

"Now wait a minute, McGurk," I said. "You mean just going around ripping off the rabbits? That would be dumber than painting them, and you said *that* was dumb."

"Yeah," said Willie. "Just a crummy carbolic copy."

"Just a crummy *carbon* copy, Willie," said Wanda. She turned to McGurk. "Those were your very words. Just a crummy carbon copy of the big gnome fight."

"Sure! Sure!" McGurk started rocking again. His eyes were wide open and gleaming now as he looked around at us. "But don't you see? All that paint business might have given Ed ideas. Stirred up the old itch. Maybe he's taken the rabbits to get them ready for some really big stunt. Like—like staging a Rabbit World Series. Or a Rabbit Olympics."

"A what?" said Willie.

"You know. Marking out some big open space as a sports arena one dark night. Say the shopping plaza. With miniature tracks and hurdles and long-jump pits and pole vaults and so on. Even a swimming pool over by the fountain."

"Wow!" said Willie.

"That would be some stunt!" I agreed.

McGurk's eyes went sly and slitty again as he smiled at Wanda.

"More Ed's style, huh, Wanda?"

She nodded.

"Well, yes—sure—but—"

"Come on, now!" McGurk drawled, still grinning, still sly. "The truth, Officer Grieg. Are *you* in on it? With him?"

She scowled.

"I—am—*not!*" she said. "I wouldn't join Ed in a game of Ping-Pong right now. Not after the way he's been acting. Mister High and Mighty. But I still don't think he left the house last night."

"All the same," said McGurk, "keep an eye on him. All right?"

"With pleasure!" she said.

"See if he's got any rabbits stashed away around the house."

"Will do!" said Wanda.

So that was *one* prime suspect. McGurk made me write it down, and before long we had a short list. Here it is:

The Great Rabbit Rip-Off
Prime Suspects
1. Ed Grieg. Motive: Material for a superstunt
2. Burt Rafferty. Motive: Same as above. Plus revenge
3. Brains Bellingham. Motive: Same as #1. Plus a challenge

One name had led to another.

For instance, Burt Rafferty's name came up because, as Wanda said:

"He must have felt so foolish, the way his painting stunt had sort of fallen flat. And out on our lawn he looked like he'd been stung when we said what a dumb idea the painting was compared to the gnome fight."

McGurk nodded, slowly rocking in time.

"True, true. . . . So you think Burt's got the same sort of idea? A *really* big stunt this time?"

"Yes," said Wanda. "Hoping to make *us* look foolish."

"Yeah!" said Willie. "And maybe get us into trouble at the same time."

"How?"

"By dumping all the rabbits in McGurk's yard one morning, and staging his stunt there. Or—or hanging them from your tree, Wanda. You know—like Christmas decorations."

We looked at each other. Willie had a good point there. That would be just like *Burt's* style, sure enough.

So I wrote down "revenge" after his name, and then chipped in with an idea of my own.

"Brains Bellingham," I said. "He's another who's always making fun of us. He's not as big a creep as

Burt, but he'd love to make the McGurk Organization look stupid."

"Oh?"

"Yes. You should have heard him yesterday. Maybe Brains has decided it's time to show us what a Master Mind he is."

"How?"

I thought about it.

"Well, if *he's* swiped the rabbits," I said, "it won't be for any Olympics set-up. No. If Brains has taken them, it'll be for something really scientific. Like piling them all into a home-made spacecraft and putting them in orbit around the church steeple."

"I'll buy that, too," said McGurk. "Put his name down." He looked around. "Any more ideas?"

We shook our heads.

"O.K.," he said. "So here's what we do next. We follow up. We investigate the prime suspects. And we keep certain facts in mind."

"Like what?" I asked.

"Like *one:* whoever took the rabbits must have snuck out in the middle of the night. And *two:* whoever took them must have stashed them away someplace."

"We know *that!*" said Wanda, impatiently. "So—"

"So listen and I'll tell you," said McGurk. "Sneaking out at that time isn't so easy for a kid. It depends on what his parents were doing. Were *they* out at a party all night? Or are they heavy sleepers? Or are they the sort who just don't worry anyway?"

"Well *my* parents—" began Wanda.

"I'm thinking about Burt's and Brains' now," said McGurk. "Those are points worth checking. Then there's the question of stashing. All those rabbits will take up a lot of room. They can't just be hidden under a guy's shirts in a drawer. We have to check on which of the suspects has access to a shed or a garage that isn't used much."

We all listened carefully. When McGurk really gets into his stride, he talks a lot of sense.

"And there's one more thing," he said. "Whoever did it would need some sort of transportation. A

shopping cart at least. And there'd probably be more than one person, to clean out the whole neighborhood like that. So that's something else to remember, when you're inquiring."

He stood up.

"Got all that?"

We nodded.

"Right. So now we split up and get to work. Wanda—you're a natural for Ed. Joey—you find out all you can about Brains. Willie—you will concentrate on Burt while I check out his buddies. Any questions?"

There weren't. We were all raring to go by now.

"O.K. Let's get on it while the trail's still hot."

We rushed to the door.

But McGurk suddenly had another idea.

"Wait!"

He had paused by the table. His hair seemed ablaze, his eyes were a bright go-go green. His head was really buzzing, you could tell.

"There *is* something else. Check to see how alert the suspects are. If they were up half the night, it'll show."

Well, after a briefing like that you'd think we'd be bound to turn *something* up, right?

Wrong!

All I could find out from a clear-eyed, ultra-alert Brains Bellingham was that he'd had an especially good sleep the night before. He'd been trying out a new invention, something he'd made from an old car radio.

"It makes white noise," he said.

"White what?"

"White *noise*. A beautiful swishing wooshing sound, like the sea coming in. You just switch it on and it masks out all other noises: aircraft, cars, dogs barking in the night, furnace noises, things like that. It gave me the best sleep I've had in months."

"Huh!" I grunted. "Suppose a burglar had broken in. You wouldn't have heard a thing and—"

"Burglars?" he said—looking very smart. "In *this*

neighborhood? Where the *McGurk* Organization lives? They wouldn't dare!"

"Don't get cute!" I said—and marched off empty-handed.

The other officers didn't have any better luck. Or at least, what they got was all negative. Burt Rafferty, for instance, had the best alibi in the world.

"He's been in bed since six o'clock last night," Willie reported.

"Oh?" said McGurk, suspiciously.

"Yes," said Willie. "Sick. With the measles. Now *he's* got little red spots all over him."

And the result of Wanda's searching in all the likely places in and around her house was the same.

"Zilch!" she said, when she reported to the basement early that afternoon. "Besides, Ed went out and jogged fifteen miles between breakfast and lunch. Dad went with him, on his bike, so I know it's true. And you don't jog fifteen miles after being up all night."

"So?" McGurk murmured.

There was something else, he could tell. In fact we could all tell. When Wanda is excited or has some special news, good or bad, she gets two spots of color the size of cherry candy-drops on her cheeks.

"So forget it anyway," she said. "It's all over!"

"You mean someone *else* has been caught?"

"Someone's confessed?"

She shook her head.

"No. But just before lunch I saw Joanne. She says all the rabbits are being replaced, free of charge. Donny is coming around now with the replacements. She says they had a whole bunch left over and Donny doesn't see why his customers should be without their rabbits, just because of a stupid joke."

"Gee!" gasped Willie. "That's really good of him! I was getting to miss my Benjie. Uh—" He blushed. "That's what I called our rabbit."

I felt the same as Willie.

"Isn't that just like old Donny?" I said. "Maybe he's hoping to *shame* the ones who did it."

"A very nice gesture," murmured Wanda.

But McGurk wasn't pleased.

"Yeah!" he snarled, slapping the desk. "Beautiful! So let's all sing hymns!" He glared around. "Don't you *see*, dummies? It makes no difference to *us*. Larceny is still larceny, even if some do-gooder replaces the property. Even if the *victim* says forget it. Anyway, I *was* a victim and I for one *don't* say forget it. A crime's a crime and we're gonna solve it. . . ."

What's *that* you're typing?" he snapped at me.

I showed him.

In the middle of the record sheet I had typed:

```
                    Case Closed
```

"Well, just erase that, Officer Rockaway, because the case *isn't* closed until we find out who ripped off those rabbits!"

I shrugged.

"You're the boss," I said, canceling the two words with a row of X's. "Besides, I need to clean my type before I use it again anyway."

"So do it later!" snarled McGurk, as I reached for my type cleaner. "Right now we've got to keep on investigating."

"Listen!"

Wanda was over by the open door. She went up two of the steps to the yard and looked out. Then she came back.

"Here's Donny now," she said. "He's just putting your replacement on the lawn."

"Good!" said McGurk, already on his way. "Let's talk to him. Maybe he *can* help us with an idea or two this time."

7 The Blushing Bloodshot Bunny

But Donny was about as helpful as before—which isn't saying much.

He was cheerful, though. His teeth shone in a wide white smile through the beard, and his cheeks and eyes had the sort of glow that doing good deeds always gives a person. At least he'd lost his worried look.

"Hey!" he said, smiling down on *McGurk's* worried look. "Why don't you drop it, man? No one's going to be the loser. We're replacing every single rabbit, free. Just let it lie, why don't you?"

"No *way!*" said McGurk, growling it out deep and firm.

Then he told Donny what he'd already told us.

Donny listened with respect, but there was still a smile shining through his beard at the end.

"You're a hard man, Lieutenant McGurk, and I wish you luck! But you're wasting your time, you know that?"

"We'll see," said McGurk, still frowning.

Wanda nudged him.

She told us later that it was to remind McGurk to say thanks for the replacement, before Donny left.

But McGurk misunderstood her. He thought she'd just had the same idea that had occurred to him.

"Oh—and Donny!" he said. "Mr. Towers!"

Donny turned at the sidewalk.

"Yes?"

"Would you mind if I just take a look inside your car?"

Even that didn't kill Donny's smile. But he frowned a little as he replied.

"Sure! Go ahead. But why?"

McGurk was already there, his head through the open window.

"Just to see how much room they take up. I'm trying to figure out exactly what sort of transportation they needed last night."

We were all looking in by now, and it was funny to see all those rabbits: the sitting ones all clustered

tightly together on one side of the back seat, the
crouching ones on the other side, and the runners
wedged together on the floor, heads up, as if they
were trying to climb the walls.

"That's only about half the total," said Donny.
"When I started out there was a trunkful as well."

McGurk nodded.

"I see. So whoever did it would certainly need
more than one cart—even if they were using those
big supermarket carts."

Donny laughed.

"Maybe they used a *van*," he said. "A stolen van
with a souped-up engine, false license plates, and a
professional wheels man to drive it."

"Uh—how's that?" said McGurk, not a bit amused.

"Well, you *know!* Maybe these rabbits are works

of art, after all. Maybe some international art thief spotted them. Maybe he figured he could sell them for a thousand dollars each to art collectors around the world. Donny Towers originals!"

Then he got into the car and drove off, with a cheerful blast of the horn.

"Big joke!" muttered McGurk.

Wanda sighed.

"Maybe we *had* better drop the case," she said.

"Yes," I said. "Because you can count on it—that's the sort of kidding we're going to be getting from everyone from now on."

McGurk shook his head angrily. He looked ready to take a flying kick at the replacement rabbit on the lawn.

"No!" he said. "We've been laughed at before. But when *we* take a case we finish it. Come on! Let's get back to the office and go over every scrap of information again. All the notes and all the facts. . . . *Willie!*"

Willie was still standing on the sidewalk, looking at Donny's car as if it was a fairy coach instead of a beat-up old Chevy. It had pulled up farther down the street.

When McGurk shouted, Willie jumped.

"Huh! What—?"

"Move it! Back to the office! We—"

"No. Wait. I'm just trying to think."

"Think? Think what?"

"Think what that smell was."

"What smell?"

"In the car. The rabbits."

"A *rabbit* smell!" jeered McGurk. "What else? Now quit the fooling and—"

"No!" cried Willie. "Wait! I've got it! It—it was a *paint remover* smell. Yes!"

We looked at one another.

"*I* didn't smell anything like that," I said. "Gasoline, maybe. It *is* an old car."

"I didn't smell paint remover, either," said McGurk. "But we don't have Willie's nose."

He was looking very serious and alert now. As I've mentioned before, McGurk is a very great believer

in Willie's sensitive nose.
So is Wanda. You could
call them real *fans* of
Willie's nose.

"Are you sure, Willie?" asked Wanda.

"Positive!" said Willie.

Now that he'd been able to name the smell, he looked almost as cheerful as Donny himself. Cheerful and relieved.

But McGurk was looking thoughtful.

"Now how about *that?*" he murmured.

And instead of continuing on his way to the basement, he turned back and picked up the replacement rabbit.

It was one of the runners. He turned it over in his hands, slowly, as if looking for chips or some other kind of flaw. Willie stuck his head closer until he nearly got his nose trapped between the ears.

"*This* smells of paint remover, too!" he cried.

"Yeah!" grunted McGurk, suddenly stopping the turning and peering at its face. "*I* can't smell it, but I sure can *see* something. Take a look, men!"

He pointed to the rabbit's cheeks. There was a faint rosiness there, as well as in the eyes.

"It's blushing!" said Wanda.

"A blushing bloodshot bunny!" I said.

"It's either the exact same one we had yesterday," said McGurk, "or one of the others that got its eyes painted."

"Yes, but—" began Willie, looking puzzled.

"And whoever tried to wipe it clean just *has* to know something about last night's job," I said.

"Do you think—?" Wanda broke off, as puzzled as Willie. "Oh, but *why?* It doesn't make sense!"

"This is just one," said McGurk. "It might be one of the three in Donny's yard. It might be that the rabbit snatchers missed it and Donny decided to use it as a replacement." He looked up. "But I'll tell you *one* thing that's sure, men."

"What's that?"

"That right now we're going to check around and see if there are any others like this. Rabbits that look as if they've had red paint removed. And if there are—and there's more than three—we'll be paying that Rabbit Factory another visit!"

8 The Return to the Rabbit Factory

There were more than three rabbits with traces of paint.

There were dozens.

"Maybe they splashed the new rabbits with paint by accident," said Wanda.

"We'll see," grunted McGurk.

So we went to the Rabbit Factory, as planned.

"Don't say anything to let them know we're suspicious," McGurk warned us, on the way. "Just keep your eyes and ears open. . . . Oh, yes—and you keep your nose open, Willie."

When we got there, three of the rabbit-makers were busy at the bench.

Donny was out. Joanne greeted us. She looked very happy this time, but in a big hurry.

"Hi!" she said. "Come on in, but please don't get in the way. We're fifteen rabbits short to make up the replacements, and we want to get them delivered by five o'clock."

Sam and Ferdie were in a more playful mood. They must have been well ahead with the production of ears and legs.

"Assume the position, Sam!" said Ferdie. "Here come the fuzz!"

Then, laughter all over their faces, they went to the wall and leaned against it with their arms and legs spread out—ready to be searched.

McGurk smiled politely, but he was in no mood for jokes. Joanne gave him a curious look.

"Still on official business, Lieutenant?" she asked, trying to kid around too, but not doing such a good job of it.

"Well, yeah," said McGurk, slowly and sadly. "But we don't seem to be getting very far. Say"—he blinked up at Joanne very innocently—"do you have any red paint around here, miss?"

"You still on *that* part of the case?" asked Joanne, over her shoulder, looking genuinely surprised.

"Well, in a way, yes, miss," McGurk replied. "We hate loose ends."

"No," said Joanne. "We don't have any red paint. Not a drop. Not even red nail polish," she added, wiggling her clayey fingers.

"Why don't you take a look around and see for yourselves," said Sam, winking at Ferdie. "Take the place apart if you like."

Well, we didn't make it as obvious as that, but we certainly did look around, in between kidding with the helpers and watching Joanne assemble the last batch of rabbits. We hadn't expected to see any cans of red paint anyway, so we weren't disappointed about that. On the other hand, we didn't see any bottles of paint remover either, and that *was* a bit of a blow.

Even so, our visit hadn't been entirely useless.

On the way back to our H.Q., McGurk said:

"Did you notice the pile of rejects and broken rabbits?"

"Yes," said Willie. "It was a lot bigger than yesterday."

"Not only bigger," I said. "But among the bits and pieces I counted seven red-painted ears and quite a lot of red eyes and legs and tails and noses."

"Right!" said McGurk. His eyes were gleaming very bright now. "Oh, they swiped those rabbits last night, I'm sure! But why?" The gleam left his eyes as he looked at us, blinking. "Why? Just to go to all the trouble of taking them back?"

I'd been thinking about this.

"Taking them back after cleaning them up, remember," I said. "Maybe Donny was more miffed about the painting than he pretended to be. Maybe he couldn't *rest* until that paint was removed."

"Yeah," said Willie. "But what about the pile of broken ones?"

"They could just have been damaged in the car," I said. "You saw the way the replacements were all crowded in the back seat. Well, last night there wouldn't have been time to pack them carefully."

McGurk nodded.

"I guess that theory *would* account for Donny and Joanne looking so upset yesterday and being so happy today."

But Wanda shook her head.

"Oh, no!" she said, very firmly. "That was because of something else. Don't tell me you didn't see it, any of you?"

"See what?"

"Joanne's ring. It's come back from repair. She wasn't wearing it, because of all the clay on her hands. But it was there, all right."

McGurk stopped.

"Where?"

"On the shelf over the bench. Out of the way. For greater safety, I suppose. It's very beautiful. I'm surprised you didn't see it sparkling."

McGurk was frowning.

Then he shrugged and began walking again.

"We've got more on our minds than women's jewelry, Officer Grieg! What we've got here is one of the very worst kinds of mysteries."

"What kind's that?" asked Willie.

McGurk spoke savagely, his eyes to the ground.

"Where we know *who's* done the crime, but we don't know *why* they did it. And if we don't know *why*, we don't have a case!"

9 "I've Solved It!"

"Why? . . . Why? . . . Why?"

That was the word used most frequently in our office during the next hour or so.

In fact it was very nearly the only word, after a while.

The best answer we'd been able to come up with was the theory that Donny hadn't liked to see his rabbits all daubed up.

"But why didn't he just go around to the houses with a bottle of paint remover and a cloth?" said Wanda. "And do it there?"

"Well, some people *liked* their rabbits painted," I said, glancing at Willie. "They might not have agreed."

"Yes, but he could have *asked*," said McGurk. "I mean, going to all that trouble to collect them in the night. It must have taken *hours*. Besides, think of the risk, with Sam and Ferdie having police records and all. If anyone had spotted them, who'd have believed they were just cruising around at two or three in the morning to pick up clay rabbits?"

I had to agree. It did seem unlikely.

Then Willie said:

"Hey! What if Sam and Ferdie did the swiping on their own? Just to keep in practice. With Donny and Joanne being shocked when they found out, and taking all the rabbits back real quick?"

That seemed even more unlikely. McGurk shot it down.

"*One*," he said, "Sam and Ferdie are supposed to be *reformed* crooks. *Two*: even if they weren't reformed, they are real professionals. A pickpocket wouldn't go around knocking off clay rabbits for practice. He'd go to the shopping plaza at the busiest time and get busy with wallets and purses. Same with Ferdie. He was a professional *car* thief."

Willie looked so put down that I said:

"They could have done it for a joke. With Donny getting scared stiff that people would take it the wrong way, knowing about Sam and Ferdie's records."

But I had to admit that it still didn't seem right—though even then I couldn't quite get rid of the feeling that Sam and Ferdie's records had *something* to do with it.

Anyway, as I say, after a while the atmosphere in McGurk's basement got very gloomy. It just seemed we were going around in circles and getting exactly nowhere.

So to do something useful and pass the time, I decided to clean my typewriter.

This time McGurk had no objections. He was still too busy trying to puzzle out the mystery, sitting back in the chair, not rocking, just glowering up at the ceiling. Only Willie was interested as I pulled out the strip of plastic and started rolling it up in a ball.

"What's that?"

"Plastic."

"It looks a little like the clay they use at the Rabbit Factory."

"It does a little," I said. "But it never sets hard, thank goodness."

"What's it for?"

"Watch and you'll see."

The plastic was nice and soft by now, so I stuck it against the type, a whole row of letters. They'd been pretty messed up with old ink, especially in the *e*'s and *a*'s and *o*'s, but when I pulled the plastic away, the dirt came with it and the letters were nice and shiny and clean.

"Hey! That's real neat!" said Willie. Then he frowned. "What happens to the ink on the plastic, though?"

"You just fold it in," I said. "Like this. . . . Then you work it in"—I started squeezing the ball of plastic again—"and the ink's swallowed up, and you're ready for another row of dirty type. Like—"

"HEY! LET ME!"

It was McGurk who had yelled, making us all jump.

He had leaped out of his chair, leaving it rocking wildly.

His hand was already grabbing at the plastic.

"Sure," I said, "but—"

"Look! Look! Watch this!" McGurk was peering at the type. Then he carefully lifted up a single letter and pressed it against the plastic. Then another letter. Then another. Then another.

I laughed.

"You don't do it one letter at a time, dummy! You do it with a whole bunch at a—"

"Who's interested in *that?*" he said. "Look! See what I've got printed on the plastic!"

He held it out.

Here's what it looked like:

"Grin?" said Willie.

Wanda gasped.

"No! *Ring!* . . . Hey, McGurk! I really think you might have got something there!"

"Got *something?*" he yelled, folding up the plastic

and making the word disappear. "I've *solved* it! I've solved it!"

He had, too.

Even without his next demonstration, I could see what he was getting at. And this time the theory did make sense.

"Look, Willie," he said. "If it's just the *word* that bothers you, let me show you with a model."

He took a paper clip out of the box. Then he twisted it around for a few seconds.

"There," he said, throwing it down on the table when he had finished. "What's that?"

"A ring," said Willie, still looking mystified. "Kind of."

"Right," said McGurk. "So let's suppose it's Joanne's ring, and this is the Rabbit Factory, and this here is a lump of the rabbit clay. Right?"

He was rolling the plastic into an egg shape.

"Now," he continued. "She takes the ring off her finger so it won't get messed up, and she lays it on one side. But then she gets so busy with the rabbit-making that she forgets it and—by accident—*plunk!*" He put the plastic on top of the paper-clip ring, covering it. "She does that with one of her hunks of clay. And they're much bigger, don't forget. O.K.?"

We nodded.

His eyes were gleaming their brightest.

"Right. Now. Remember what happened to Joey's pencil yesterday. The ring does the same. It sticks to the bottom of the clay—like this."

He lifted the plastic and of course the "ring" went up with it.

"Then she gets on with molding the clay into shape and—*zapp!*—the ring gets swallowed. Inside the rabbit's body."

He made the paper-clip ring disappear the same way.

Then he looked around, shining with triumph.

There was a pause while we thought about it.

"So you figure that would account for the rabbits being rounded up last night?" I said. "Donny and Joanne suddenly realized what had happened. They were anxious to get the ring back but they didn't know which rabbit had it."

"It all fits, doesn't it?" said McGurk.

"You bet!" cried Willie. "McGurk, you've done it again!"

And he clapped, and who could blame him?

But Wanda still wasn't quite sure.

"But—wouldn't Joanne miss the ring at the end of the session? When she washed up?"

"Sure!" cried McGurk. "But she wouldn't know where it had gone. At first she'd just look around on the floor, under the bench, thinking it had gotten brushed off." He frowned knowingly. "And I bet she did it secretly, too!"

"Why?"

"Because at first she'd be scared to mention it. She wouldn't want Donny to think she'd been so careless with the ring he'd given her."

"That figures," said Wanda.

Then she shook her head. "But Donny *knew* about it. *He* pretended it had gone for repair, too, don't forget."

"Yes," said McGurk, "but that was after she hadn't been able to find it. After she'd *had* to tell him that it was missing."

I nodded rapidly.

"Yes. But she only told *him*, I bet. They wouldn't mention it to Sam and Ferdie at first."

"Why not?" said Willie. "They could have helped to look for it."

"They did in the *end*," I said. "But at first I bet Donny and Joanne—"

"*Suspected that either Sam or Ferdie had stolen it. Yes!*" boomed a voice from the doorway. "I'm ashamed to say that's exactly what we *did* think!"

It was Donny himself. Joanne was right behind him. They were standing at the open door. We'd been so excited we hadn't heard them arrive.

Joanne was carrying a huge gray egg tied with a red silk ribbon.

10 The Egg

"Sorry!" said Joanne, when we'd asked them inside. "But we couldn't help hearing. We were on our way to reward you and—"

"*Reward* us?" said McGurk.

"Yes," said Donny, grinning through his beard.

"For what?"

"For putting us on the right track yesterday. We were awfully worried. Not just because of the missing ring, but mainly because it looked as if either Sam or Ferdie or both had been slipping back into their old ways."

"I can understand that," said Wanda, looking at McGurk. "It's just what I said right at the start. Step out of line in a big way once—just once—and everyone suspects you when something like it happens again."

"It's what is called giving a dog a bad name," said Donny.

"But then you four came around to the garage," said Joanne. "And you lost your pencil, Joey, and you spotted it, Willie, under that lump of clay. And then we saw at once that that could easily have happened to the ring."

"Boy, were we relieved!" said Donny, tugging at his beard. "But of course we still had a problem."

"Yes." Joanne thoughtfully fingered the bow on the ribbon around the egg. I saw now that it was made of clay, like the rabbits. "The problem was: *which rabbit had swallowed the ring?*"

"But at least we were able to discuss it with Sam and Ferdie at last, and tell them what had happened."

"I suppose we could just have announced it publicly," said Joanne, frowning. "And then gone around breaking up the rabbits house by house. Giving the owners replacements on the spot."

"Ah!" cried McGurk. "That would have been stupid! It—"

"Exactly what Sam and Ferdie said," Donny chipped in. "And I had to agree. Too risky."

"But why would it have been too risky?" asked Wanda. "*I'd* have been glad to break open *our* rabbit. I'd have helped you at the other houses, as well."

"Me too," said Willie. "Uh—only I'd have asked you to leave Benjie till the last."

"*I'll* tell her why it was too risky," said McGurk, before Donny or Joanne could explain. He gave Wanda and Willie a scornful look. "Sam and Ferdie were right. If people got to know there might be a valuable ring inside their rabbits, some of them would want it for themselves. They'd take the rabbits indoors and pretend they'd given them away or something. Then they'd crack them open in private."

Donny laughed uneasily.

"Well," he said, "I myself have a higher opinion of the people around here. But they might have been *tempted,* and we wouldn't have wanted that. Anyway, as Sam pointed out, it wouldn't be the customers who'd be the main risk. He said that if the word got out it would spread like fire, and then there might be real thieves from all over town coming to grab the rabbits."

"So we just kept it secret and collected them ourselves," said Joanne.

McGurk nodded. He was looking a bit annoyed with himself at that moment.

"And we might have known it right at the beginning, men! Someone with a car. Adults, free to go out in the middle of the night." He sighed, then gave Donny a crafty grin. "But tell me this. How many rabbits did you have to bust before you found the ring? *Fifteen*, right?"

"Good shot!" said Donny. "But eighteen, in fact, counting our own three, which were the first to go. And I guess we were lucky. Imagine if we hadn't found it until the very last rabbit of all! We'd be slaving away yet, making replacements."

"It took us long enough to get the paint off the ones we didn't smash," said Joanne.

"Uh—yes," said McGurk. "That reminds me. Why *did* you bother to clean them up?"

Donny tugged at his beard. His own cheeks were going red. He smiled sheepishly.

"Well, if we'd returned painted rabbits, it would

have looked funny. They had to look like entirely new replacements. We just didn't want people to know what had really happened. We wouldn't want them to get the wrong idea. That we didn't trust them."

"Like you, McGurk!" said Wanda, giving him a hard look.

But McGurk had an answer for that.

"Sure," he said. "But look what would have happened if Donny and Joanne had managed to cover up, just to spare people's feelings. Innocent people would still have been suspected of taking the rabbits. Like you and your brother, and Burt Rafferty, and Brains Bellingham, and even Sam and Ferdie. You've just *got* to follow a case like this through to the end."

"He's right," sighed Donny. "The Lieutenant is absolutely right."

"You bet I am!" growled McGurk.

"Anyway," said Joanne, placing the egg on the table, "here's the reward. Donny was out getting the ribbon for it when you stopped by. I'd have explained everything then, only I didn't want to spoil the surprise."

"From all of us at the Rabbit Factory to all of you," said Donny.

They left then, in a hurry, saying they were late for a party.

McGurk picked up the egg in both hands.

"Heavy," he murmured. "I wonder what—"

He gave it a shake.

There was a crisp rattling sound from inside.

"Why don't you open it?" said Wanda.

"Yeah, but how?"

"You'll just have to break it, McGurk. Like those eighteen rabbits," I said.

"It's what eggs are *for*," said Wanda.

"Uh—can I have the ribbon?" said Willie. "For my new rabbit's neck."

"Sure," said McGurk.

So he took the ribbon off, gave it to Willie, then gently bounced the egg on the floor.

"Harder!" we urged. "Put some muscle into it!"

It broke on the third bounce. The hard clay split

open and a shower of brightly wrapped candy and other objects spilled out in a shaft of sunlight, where they glittered like treasure.

There was a big card in with them:

A Happy Easter
to

The McGurk Organization
— with thanks & admiration

from

Joanne, Dorny, Sam
& Ferdie
and all the rabbits !

Even without Sam's name on the card we would have known that the ex-Super-Dip had had a hand in the gift. A very skillful hand. It didn't take a detective to see that.

Why?

Because of those "other objects."

"Hey!" cried Wanda, picking something out from the candy with one hand and digging into her jeans pocket with the other. "This is my lucky seashell!"

"Yeah!" Willie was staring popeyed at the object he'd picked up. "And this is my Canadian dime!"

"And my spare pencil!" I yelled.

As for McGurk, the object he pounced on was his own ID card. Again!

But he didn't mind.

Once more the Organization had cracked a case. And when that happens, nothing can upset McGurk—but *nothing!*

"By the way," he said, as we crouched over the candy. "Did I tell you that the candy yesterday was an Easter gift to the Organization from Mrs. Emmet?"

"No, you did not!" said Wanda, indignantly.

"But it explains another mystery," I murmured.

I'd been wondering how come McGurk had been so generous with his own candy. It usually takes a miracle to get him to give just one little chocolate-covered peanut away.

"Well, I thought that since they were the Organization's property, it would be a good way of using them," he said. "Official business. But now the Great Rabbit Rip-Off has been solved, we can celebrate with *this* candy. Dig in, men!"

And he didn't even wait to divvy up—just grabbed

two fistfuls of the best he could see. Two whole fistfuls of Payments for Information Leading to an
Arrest.

It looked a bit greedy,
but what the heck.

I guess he'd earned the
lion's share this time.

E

The gr   t   r
rip-of

DATE			
NOV 2 1 1978	JAN 2 5 1979	MAR 7 1980	
DEC 9 1978	FEB 1 6 1979		1980
JAN 2 0 1978	MAR 1 1979	APR 1980	1980
FEB 1 7 1978	APR 5 1979	APR 1 1980	
MAR 1 7 1978	APR 1 9 1979		
MAY 2 5 1978	MAY 1 0 1979		
OCT 2 1978	MAY 1 8 1979		
OCT 2 0 1978	MAY 2 2 1979		
NOV 2 0 1978	OCT 2 2 1979		
DEC 5 1978	NOV 5 1979		
DEC 2 2 1978	DEC 2 1 1979		